This book belongs to:

_____

Bleu, his mother and best friend Piper

1

Thank you to:

Pati Sato, Andy Johnson, Melissa Chandler, Olivia Nason, Brian VanHorn, Nancy MacDonald, Tammy Boucher, Teresa Downey, John Carroll, Susan Laughlin, Bettye Skeoch, Curious Bleu, his mom, Laverne, and the entire Miles Smith Farm cattle herd and my colleagues at HP for putting up with my farm stories.

Publisher: Miles Smith Farm
56 Whitehouse Road, Loudon, NH 03307

ISBN # 978-0-9887297-0-4

Printed in the United States of America
Town and Country Reprographics, Concord, NH
First Edition December 2012
Second Edition December 2012
Third Edition February 2013
Fourth Edition March 2013
Fifth Edition April 2013

The Curious Little Calf Named Bleu

Curious Bleu Finds His Moo

Written by Carole Soule
Illustrated by Issa Nyaphaga

The Curious Little Calf Named Bleu

It is early September on Miles Smith Farm and the cattle are busy eating leaves and grass. The days are getting cooler. The calves love to play and run together.

There is a pack of coyotes who live in the forest nearby. Sometimes at night the coyotes visit Farmer Bruce's field. From the house Farmer Bruce can hear them howling.

The cows have big horns and the coyotes are afraid of them. Whenever the cows are around the calves are safe.

5

At midnight, on a full moon called a "Blue Moon," Laverne had a little baby boy calf. She named him Bleu. He drank his mother's milk. When his belly was full he grew sleepy.

His mother nuzzled him and told him what a good boy he was. Bleu loved his mother because she made him feel safe and loved.

The next morning Farmer Bruce said to his wife, Carole, "Look, Laverne finally had her calf. We should check out the new baby."

While the farmers were busy with morning chores, Bleu learned how to stand. On wobbly legs, he learned to walk, run and play. Running made him happy.

Bleu's mother had not told him about farmers. When Farmer Carole walked into the field he was afraid and ran under the fence, over the stone wall and into the forest.

Bleu ran far into the forest.

When he stopped he was alone. He could not see his mother and was scared. Tired, he curled up in soft pile of dried leaves.

"Get off my acorns. You are lying on my acorns. Get off!" said Jerald the chipmunk.

Bleu looked down and saw a chipmunk pulling at something under his leg.

"Who are you?" Bleu asked.

"Never mind," the chipmunk said. "Just get off my acorns. I have to collect them before winter. Will you just move?"

Bleu moved his leg and watched as the chipmunk picked up an acorn.

"I'm looking for my mother." Bleu asked, "Have you seen her?"

"No, I have not seen your mother. I am busy getting ready for the winter. Try calling to her."

"Call to her? How can I do that?" asked Bleu.

"When I was little and got scared, I called to my mother by chirping," Jerald said.

"How do I chirp?" asked Bleu.

The chipmunk said, "Like this." He raised his head and made the sound of chirp, chirp.

Bleu tried to chirp.

All the noise got the attention of the chipmunk's wife who scurried over to see what was going on.

"Jerald, what are you doing? Where are those acorns?" asked Jeraldine. Jerald looked at Bleu and said,

"Maybe chirping isn't for you. You should ask Groundhog what to do. He can help you. I have to get back to work. Good luck."

Jerald and Jeraldine hurried off.

13

Bleu jumped to his feet. Looking around, he didn't see anyone. "Where was that voice coming from," he wondered. "Should I run?"

Then a nose poked up from the ground. A furry face, followed by a round little body, emerged.

"Hruumpf. You don't look dangerous. Why are you making that racket?"

"Sorry," Bleu said. "Are you Groundhog?"

Bleu got up, still trying to chirp like the chipmunk. Bleu walked further into the woods. He was alone and scared. He sat down and started to cry.

"Who's making all that racket? Be quiet."

14

"Who wants to know?"

"My name is Bleu. I'm alone and can't find my mother. I don't know how to chirp to call her."

"Chirp! Only chipmunks and birds chirp." Groundhog waddled closer. "When you are in trouble, squeal. That's what groundhogs do when they need help." The forest filled with a loud squeal.

"Now you try," said Groundhog.

Bleu took a big breath and tried to squeal. He tried and tried but the only noise he made sounded like rustling leaves. Bleu knew he couldn't squeal like the groundhog. He sat down with a thud and cried.

"Oh! There's that awful racket," said Groundhog reaching to cover his ears.

"I can't help it. I can't call to my mother," said Bleu in between sobs.

"Hruumpf," said Groundhog, "You'd

better find some place to go soon. It's getting dark and the coyotes will be out."

That only made Bleu cry more.

"Quiet now. Let me think what we can do," said Groundhog.

Closing his eyes, Groundhog sat very still while he thought. His whiskers twitched and his ears wiggled.

He sat there for a long time before he said, "The only warm, safe place for me at night is underground. I have a big den. Why don't you stay with me?"

"Okay." Bleu poked his nose into Groundhog's hole.

Groundhog pushed and pushed but Bleu could not fit.

"Hruumpf, hruumpf. Don't worry. Digging is what I do best. I'll dig a hole for you to lie down in. Covering you with leaves and loose dirt will keep you warm and safe."

It was dark when Groundhog finished. He then scurried into his own hole.

"But I'm hungry," cried out Bleu before falling into an exhausted sleep.

The next morning, Groundhog stuck his head out and said, "Good morning, Bleu. Were you safe and warm in that hole?"

Bleu said, "Yes, thank you, Mr. Groundhog. But now I'm hungry and want to find my mother."

Groundhog grumbled and snorted. He closed his eyes and twitched his whiskers then said, "I've seen animals like you. They live past my garden. I'll show you the way."

Off they went with Groundhog waddling up a long hill in front of Bleu. "Here is my garden. Keep walking along this road," said Groundhog.

Bleu walked along the road. Ahead two young bulls were wrestling in a pasture.

Bleu watched the bulls wrestle.

"Hey, who are you? And what are you doing outside the fence?" said one bull.

"I'm looking for my mother," Bleu said.

"Hey Jake, wasn't that cow in the next field calling for someone?" said Fred.

"Stu or Lou? It was Bleu! The name was Bleu," Jake bellowed.

"That's my name! That must be my mother! Where is she?"

Jake pointed his horn toward the stone wall. Bleu ran over the wall.

He saw his mother in the next field. She was calling to him.

Bleu was so excited, he yelled, "Mooother, Mooother!"

When his mother, Laverne, saw Bleu, she kicked up her heels and ran to meet him.

She nuzzled and rubbed Bleu with her nose and said, "Welcome home, I missed you."

"Mommy, I can call you now." Bleu shouted, "Mooother. Mooother. Moo. Moo."

23

Farmer Bruce heard the cows mooing. He said, "Look, Carole, that little calf is back. How did he survive in the forest without his mother? I think his curiosity leads him to trouble but maybe helped him get back, too."

It's all about coming home to family, friends and safe pastures.

Fun Facts

1 Both male and female Scottish Highlander cattle have horns. Typically the male horns grow down and the female horns grow up, although this is not always the case.

2 Cattle drink about 10 gallons of water a day. Lactating cows (cows with nursing calves) drink about 20 gallons of water a day.

3 Scottish Highlanders grow long shaggy coats to help protect them from winter weather. Cows with shaggy coats need shade to help manage heat stress in warm weather.

4 Scottish Highlander cattle are beef cattle, a heritage breed imported since the 1880's. A cow will produce just enough milk for her calf. Beef cattle typically are not milked.

5 The gestation period for a cow, including Scottish Highlanders, is 9 months. Ideally, calves are born in the spring so they have all summer with their mothers on pasture before they are weaned.

6 Miles Smith Farm raises both Scottish Highlander and Angus Cross cattle. Curious Bleu is a Scottish Highlander calf.

Photo taken by Oumarou
Mebouack

Issa Nyaphaga

Issa Nyaphaga is a multimedia artist and illustrator living in the US. He is internationally known as an activist and political cartoonist and has collaborated with various well-known established institutions and artists around the world. In the 1990's, he published over 7,000 cartoons, drawings, illustrations, graphic novels and comics in his home country of Cameroon, reaching 5,000,000 readers. Since 1999, Issa has taught his art techniques in universities, cultural centers and social institutes. He also conducts Art Therapy programs for child soldiers, children-at-risk and teenagers. Issa divides his time between Africa, China, France and the United States where he shares his work and advice with young artists. Issa lives in Santa Fe, NM. For more info: www.nyaphaga.com.

Illustrator & Bleu

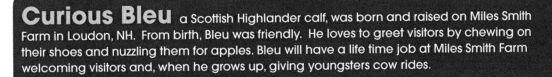

Curious Bleu

a Scottish Highlander calf, was born and raised on Miles Smith Farm in Loudon, NH. From birth, Bleu was friendly. He loves to greet visitors by chewing on their shoes and nuzzling them for apples. Bleu will have a life time job at Miles Smith Farm welcoming visitors and, when he grows up, giving youngsters cow rides.

27

Photo taken by Geoff Forester

Author

Carole Soule Carole Soule and her husband, Bruce Dawson, are escapees from the high tech world where they were both software programmers. They started with a herd of two black Scottish Highlander cattle in 2002 and today have over 65 head of Highlanders and Angus cross cattle on Miles Smith Farm. The farm was founded in the 1830's by Miles Smith, who now resides, with most of his family, in an on-farm cemetery. Both Carole and Bruce are committed to sustainable and local living as well as humane treatment of cattle. They sell the beef and other locally produced products in an on-farm retail store in Loudon, NH. Committed to educating the public about farm life, they hope that this story about a curious calf will inspire parents and children to learn more about the mysteries and joys of living with cattle. Learn more about their cattle and Curious Bleu's adventures at www.milessmithfarm.com or at Miles Smith Farm's Facebook page. Through education and collaboration, we can enhance the lives of all.

Made in the USA
Middletown, DE
26 September 2023

38801425R00018